THE NEW
Bobbsey Twins

#10
Twins™

THE CHOCOLATE-COVERED CLUE

LAURA LEE HOPE
ILLUSTRATED BY PAUL JENNIS

A MINSTREL® BOOK

PUBLISHED BY POCKET BOOKS

New York   London   Toronto   Sydney   Tokyo

A MINSTREL PAPERBACK *ORIGINAL*

A Minstrel Book, published by
POCKET BOOKS, a division of Simon & Schuster Inc.
1230 Avenue of the Americas, New York, NY 10020

Copyright © 1989 by Simon & Schuster Inc.
Cover art copyright © 1989 Linda Thomas
Produced by Mega-Books of New York, Inc.

ISBN: 0-671-63073-3

First Minstrel Books printing February 1989

10 9 8 7 6 5 4 3 2

THE NEW BOBBSEY TWINS is a trademark of Simon & Schuster Inc.

THE BOBBSEY TWINS, A MINSTREL BOOK and colophon are registered trademarks of Simon & Schuster Inc.

Printed in the U.S.A.

Contents

1
Something's Cooking

"Double-Double Chocolate Chunkies," Flossie Bobbsey heard a soft voice purring in her ear. She was half asleep and couldn't be sure if she was dreaming.

"Peanut Butter Fudge Dreamies with lemon swirl icing," came another voice.

Flossie was almost certain the second voice belonged to her twin brother, Freddie. Yuck, she thought, why am I dreaming about him?

Suddenly the voices got louder.

"Jelly doughnuts."

"Gingerbread men with candy icing."

"Pummmmmmpernickel."

Flossie opened her eyes. Her brothers and sister were leaning over her bed.

"Wake up," Freddie said. "It's three-thirty in the morning." His blond hair was mussed, and his blue eyes were only half open.

"Just a few more minutes." Flossie moaned and tried to pull the covers over her head.

"Come on, Floss," said Bert Bobbsey. "Get up so I can go back to sleep."

Bert was Flossie's older brother. He was twelve years old, with dark brown hair and brown eyes.

Nan, Bert's twin, flopped across the foot of the bed. "That's right," she mumbled. "This is your chance to see how they make those goodies."

"Okay, okay. I'm awake." Flossie sat up slowly and rubbed her eyes.

Freddie shook Flossie's bed as hard as he could. "Come on. The Bakers will be here in half an hour. You have to get up."

Flossie grabbed her pillow and tried to hit Freddie.

"Wait a minute," he yelled as he jumped out of the way. "You said to wake you up. You didn't say how!"

"Keep it down, you two," said Bert. "We don't want to wake Mom."

"Yeah," said Freddie. "She's been working real hard on the North Side burglar story. That crook has robbed five houses in five days."

2

"That's pretty amazing, all right." Nan sat up. "But I'm too sleepy to think about it now. Besides, Flossie's new friend will be here soon."

"What's her name?" Bert asked Flossie.

"Casey Baker," Flossie said. She put down her pillow and pushed back the covers. "Her parents own—"

"Baker's Bakery," Bert interrupted. "The best bakery in Lakeport."

"I still don't believe it," Freddie grumbled. "Casey transfers to our school, and who's the first person she makes friends with?"

"I didn't plan this," Flossie said. "It just happened."

"We know that, Floss," said Nan. "And it's great that her parents offered to show you how they bake everything."

"Yeah," Freddie muttered. "Just great."

"Well, have fun," said Bert, rubbing his eyes. "We're going back to bed."

"And don't forget," Freddie said, "you promised to bring me something really delicious if I got you up on time."

"I won't forget," Flossie said.

"Good," said Freddie. "I'll see you later in school." He and the others stumbled out of the room.

Flossie gave a huge yawn, then looked at the rain pouring down her window. "The things I do for a double fudge brownie," she said. Slowly she crawled out of bed.

Flossie was ready when Casey and her parents arrived to pick her up. The drive to the bakery was quick, and by five o'clock the shop was alive with activity. The Bakers and their two assistants were preparing for a busy day.

"This place is so big," said Flossie. She and Casey were standing in the front of the shop.

The bakery was decorated with mirrors and shiny white tiles. Two long glass display cases were on one side of the room. Along the opposite wall stood a few small tables and chairs, so customers could have pastries and drinks right in the shop.

"We bake everything in the kitchen," said Casey. She peered into one of the mirrors and fluffed up her curly brown hair. "Then we bring it all out here."

"I know," said Flossie cheerfully. "I've been here with my mother." She pointed to a row of shelves on the wall behind the glass cases. "You fill those with breads and doughnuts and cakes." There was a hungry look on her face.

"You forgot the tarts, pies, and crumb cakes," Casey reminded her.

Flossie took a deep breath. "Can we go into the kitchen? I smell chocolaty things cooking."

"Sure we can," Casey said eagerly. "It's my favorite place."

She carefully pushed open one of the double doors that led to the kitchen and hurried through. Flossie was right on her heels.

The Bakers' kitchen was almost as large as the front of the bakery. Shiny baking pans of different shapes and sizes filled the shelves that lined one wall.

Flossie looked around the busy kitchen. One assistant was rolling out dough on a long marble-topped table. The other worker was carrying freshly baked bread to a rack, so it could cool.

Mr. Baker, a short man with thinning brown hair and a small mustache, was arranging cookie dough on a big silvery tray. He wore a big white apron over his clothes.

Mrs. Baker was also short, with reddish brown hair. She pushed her gold-rimmed glasses up on her nose, then poured a pitcher of milk into one of three large mixing bowls.

"Wow!" Flossie exclaimed. "Those are the biggest electric mixers I've ever seen." Each mixer was taller than Flossie, and the bowls were big enough for her to sit in.

"Who gets to lick the bowls?" Flossie asked.

"I do—sometimes," said Casey. "But I can't lick the whole thing."

"I don't think anybody could," said Flossie. She couldn't believe her eyes. All the bakery equipment was so large—even the oven.

"We can bake over one hundred cookies, all at the same time," Mr. Baker explained. He put a tray full of sugar cookies in the oven, then went into the front of the shop.

"This is great!" said Flossie. She lifted her head and took a deep breath. The sweet, warm air was filled with a dozen wonderful smells.

Then Flossie noticed Mrs. Baker. She was checking the creamy batter in one of the mixers.

"Mom's in charge of the cakes today," Casey said proudly. "Each mixer is making a different kind of cake."

"That's right," said Mrs. Baker. "Chocolate, angel food, and carrot. I have enough batter to make four of each—twelve in all."

"Twelve cakes!" Flossie's eyes lit up. "Will all of them be ready today?"

"Of course," Mrs. Baker said. "They'll be baked, cooled, iced, and ready to sell by eight o'clock this morning."

"Come on," said Casey. "I'll show you the storeroom where we keep our supplies."

"Okay," said Flossie. She followed Casey toward two large doors in the back of the kitchen. "Which door is it?" she asked.

"The one on the left," Casey replied. "The other door goes to the alley. Only delivery people use that door."

"I'm coming with you," said Mrs. Baker. "I have to get a few things anyway."

Flossie was amazed when they entered the storeroom. It was filled with sacks of flour and sugar. Neatly stacked in one corner were the spices: cinnamon, nutmeg, and ginger.

"When you make as many cakes and cookies as we do," Mrs. Baker explained, "you need large amounts of all the ingredients."

Mrs. Baker picked up several containers of spices and led the girls back into the kitchen. Then she went into the front of the store to help her husband and their assistants set up the baked goods.

"Ooh," said Casey, rubbing her arms. "All of a sudden, it's chilly in here."

Flossie felt it too. She looked around and saw that the door to the alley was open.

"I guess a delivery man must have come in while we were in the storeroom," said Flossie. "See, there are wet footprints on the floor."

"You're right," Casey agreed.

Both girls looked outside to see if anyone was there, but they couldn't see a thing.

"It's so dark out there," said Casey.

"That's because of the rain," Flossie said. She

shivered a little from the cold as she closed the door. "Should I lock it?" she asked.

"Oh, no," said Casey. "We never lock it when we're in the store."

Just then Mrs. Baker came hurrying into the kitchen. "It's time to get this chocolate cake batter into the oven."

She grabbed some cake pans and headed over to the three mixers. When she reached the first one, a puzzled expression appeared on her face.

"I must be forgetful this morning," she said.

"Why, Mom?" asked Casey.

"Because I don't remember turning this machine off." Mrs. Baker shrugged her shoulders. "Oh, well. If you girls would bring over a few more pans, I can get started."

The two girls were about to grab some pans when they heard a high-pitched wail.

"That's a police siren," Flossie cried out. "And it's right outside!"

Mrs. Baker and the two girls ran to a window that looked out onto a side street.

Through the pouring rain they caught a glimpse of a police car speeding around the corner. Its red and blue lights were flashing.

"Wow!" said Casey. "They must be after someone."

"They'll get 'em!" Flossie declared. "Lakeport has the best police in the world.

Even though," she added, "Bert, Nan, Freddie, and I have to help them out sometimes."

"Excuse me," said Mrs. Baker, wrapping her arms around the girls' shoulders. "But we have goodies to bake. Remember, you can't eat 'em if we don't bake 'em."

By seven-thirty Flossie and Casey were staring at a beautiful chocolate layer cake. It was sitting on one of the tables in the bakery. The cake was covered with rich chocolate icing and was topped with a bright red cherry.

"I've always dreamed of a cake like this," Flossie said breathlessly. She and Casey were alone in the front of the store. "Couldn't we have a teeny tiny piece?"

Casey smiled. "Remember what my mom said. There are three more being decorated in the kitchen—and one of them is being delivered to your house this afternoon."

"That's great!" Flossie exclaimed. "That means dessert will be—"

But before Flossie could finish speaking, the front door to the shop burst open. Flossie and Casey looked up in time to see a short man in a hooded mask rushing toward them.

As he reached the table, his gloved hands shot out. Flossie screamed—the hooded figure was reaching right for her!

2
Sticky Fingers

The hands were only inches away. Flossie was too scared to move a muscle.

But she was surprised by what the masked man did next. He reached past her and grabbed the chocolate layer cake right off the table. Before the girls could say a word, the thief dashed out of the shop.

"Come on," shouted Flossie. She grabbed Casey and ran after the man. But when they reached the street, he was nowhere in sight.

"We lost him," said Casey.

Flossie shivered as she looked up and down the block. Most of the stores were still closed, and the street was almost deserted. The only place that looked busy was the bus depot across the street. Flossie could see people going in and out through the revolving doors.

"I know everybody likes our cakes," said Casey. "But stealing them is really weird."

"Let's go," said Flossie as she ran back into the shop. "We've got to tell your parents now!"

Five minutes later, the girls finished telling their story to a puzzled Mr. and Mrs. Baker.

"I don't understand it," said Mr. Baker, shaking his head. "But I'm glad you two weren't hurt."

"So am I," said Mrs. Baker. She gently squeezed Casey's and Flossie's hands.

"Maybe we should call the police," Casey suggested. She looked very nervous.

"Or my brothers and sister," Flossie added.

"I don't think so," Mr. Baker said calmly. "If the man wanted a chocolate cake that badly— he can have it."

"Now, I've prepared a good hot breakfast for you," said Mrs. Baker.

"Blueberry tarts?" Flossie asked eagerly.

Mrs. Baker chuckled. "After your cereal and fruit. You need a healthy breakfast first."

"Right," Mr. Baker agreed. "So eat up, then I'll drive you both to school."

The two girls sat down at one of the tables and began eating.

Even though the food was delicious, Flossie

couldn't stop thinking about the robbery. Two questions kept racing through her mind. Who was that masked man? And why would he steal a chocolate cake, no matter how good it was?

Flossie couldn't wait to tell Freddie and the others that a really strange crook was in town. Lakeport had a cakenapper.

It was lunchtime before Flossie had a chance to talk to Freddie.

"That's really weird," said Freddie when Flossie had finished her story. He was busily picking lettuce from his tuna-fish sandwich. "Why would anybody steal a chocolate cake?"

"I don't know," said Flossie. "Maybe it was some kind of dumb joke. Anyway, the Bakers didn't seem mad about it. Mrs. Baker even gave Casey and me a wonderful piece of blueberry tart and—"

"Stop!" Freddie exclaimed. "I don't want to hear any more about all the great stuff you ate!"

Flossie's eyes sparkled mischievously. "You don't want to hear about the three different cakes they were making?"

"No."

"Or the cinnamon twist or the apple pies—"

"No, I don't," Freddie said firmly. "And besides—you didn't bring anything for me."

"I told you they're delivering a chocolate

layer cake to our house today. It might even be there already."

Freddie didn't say anything. He just stared at his sandwich. He was trying to imagine it as a big, delicious slice of chocolate layer cake.

It wasn't working.

At three-thirty that afternoon, Freddie was still thinking about cakes and other goodies.

Mrs. Bobbsey had picked up Freddie and Flossie after school. She had planned to take the younger twins with her while she ran some errands, but they wanted to go right home. Flossie wanted to relax in front of the TV. Freddie wanted a piece of chocolate layer cake.

"Mrs. Green," Freddie shouted as the three Bobbseys entered through the front door. "Did Baker's Bakery deliver a chocolate cake?"

"Yes, they did," came a voice from the dining room. Mrs. Green was the Bobbseys' part-time housekeeper. Three times a week she cleaned their house and fixed their dinner. At the moment she was busy dusting the dining-room table.

"Great!" Freddie exclaimed.

"And no one can touch it until *after* dinner," said Mrs. Green, without looking up.

"Not even a teeny tiny piece?" asked Flossie.

Mrs. Green stopped her dusting. She was a

heavyset woman with graying red hair and bright, green eyes. "Not even a piece the size of a dime," she said. "And don't let me catch you trying to sneak any."

"Mrs. Green is right," said Mrs. Bobbsey. "That cake is for dessert."

Flossie stole a look at Freddie. "I guess *I* can wait. Especially since I ate those delicious—"

"Mom," Freddie said quickly, "can I help you run your errands?"

Mrs. Bobbsey was a little surprised. "Yes, if you really want to. But I'm not going to the toy store or the computer store."

"That's okay," Freddie said. "As long as I don't have to hear any more about dessert."

Flossie leaned in close to her twin. "Not even about the dark fudge brownies with—"

Freddie turned and stomped out the door.

"You've been a lot of help," Mrs. Bobbsey said to Freddie an hour later. Both of them were carrying large packages. "I haven't had time to shop lately. Not with your father away on business and me working on my latest news story."

Mr. Bobbsey ran a large home-improvement center and lumberyard. Mrs. Bobbsey was a part-time reporter for the *Lakeport News*.

"You mean the North Side burglar story?"

Freddie asked. He stumbled along the sidewalk. He was carrying a huge bedspread, and he could barely see where he was going.

"That's the one." They reached the car, and Mrs. Bobbsey opened the back door for him. "He struck again early this morning. That makes six houses in *six* days. The police have a few suspects but no solid leads."

"I bet—we could—catch him," Freddie grunted as he pushed the package into the car.

"Let's not find out, sweetheart," Mrs. Bobbsey said. "Let the police do their job. Okay?"

"Well . . ." said Freddie.

"Good," said Mrs. Bobbsey as they slid into the front seat. "Now, for being such a help, I'll buy you a *little* something. What will it be? A new Micro-Man adventure book? A computer magazine? You can have anything you want."

"Anything?" Freddie raised an eyebrow.

"Anything," Mrs. Bobbsey replied.

Slowly Freddie began to smile. He knew exactly what he wanted his mother to buy him.

A short while later, Freddie and Mrs. Bobbsey were entering the Flying Saucer Diner.

"Remember," said Mrs. Bobbsey as they sat down at the counter. "If you have this cake now, you don't get any for dessert."

"That's okay, Mom," Freddie said cheerfully.

"But how will you feel watching the rest of us eating cake tonight?"

"Don't worry." Freddie waved at the waitress, trying to get her attention. "I'll take Chief for a walk after dinner. It's my turn anyway."

Chief was the newest member of the Bobbsey family. He was a big, shaggy, brown-and-white sheepdog puppy—clumsy, friendly, and always getting into mischief.

When the waitress came over, Mrs. Bobbsey ordered a cup of tea. Freddie eagerly ordered a slice of chocolate cake and a glass of milk.

"Coming right up, cutie," said the waitress. She popped her gum and winked at Freddie. "Baker's Bakery delivered a fresh chocolate cake this afternoon. I bet there's a slice with your name on it."

Freddie watched the waitress walk over to a display case filled with all kinds of desserts. She took the cake out and placed it on the counter. Then she went to get a knife.

Freddie sat there, tapping his fork. All he could think of was that soft, spongy center and sweet chocolate frosting.

Then a scream interrupted his daydream.

Freddie whirled around in time to see a customer pointing toward the entrance. A short man, wearing a mask, had run through the front door and was heading across the room.

When he reached the counter, he began smashing the chocolate cake with his bare hands.

One or two customers started toward him. But he instantly threw huge pieces of cake right in their faces. Then he grabbed what was left of the cake and headed for the door.

"It's the Cakenapper!" Freddie leaped from the stool and started after him.

"Freddie!" yelled Mrs. Bobbsey. "Come back here!"

Freddie didn't stop. He was determined to catch this crook. But the Cakenapper saw him coming and threw a hunk of cake at him.

Freddie dove to the floor as the chocolate mush went whizzing over his head. He looked behind him and saw a customer sitting at a table. There was chocolate cake all over the man's face.

Freddie quickly turned back toward the front door. The Cakenapper was gone.

When Freddie reached the door, he caught a glimpse of a dark car speeding away from the diner. But before he could get a better look, it disappeared into the misty autumn afternoon.

At five-thirty, all the Bobbsey twins were standing around their kitchen. Bert and Nan had come home and found Flossie asleep on the

couch. When they'd awakened her, she told them about the bakery cake theft.

Then Freddie and Mrs. Bobbsey arrived. After their mother had gone upstairs, Freddie began to tell about his adventure.

". . . And there were all those people trying to get the cake frosting out of their hair," said Freddie, finishing his story. "It was funny—kind of," he added.

"I bet Mom wasn't laughing," said Bert.

"She was too," Freddie insisted. "Well, after she finished yelling at me for chasing the guy."

"This is getting stranger by the minute," said Nan. "First the robbery at the bakery, now this one at the diner. I wonder—"

Just then the phone rang.

"I'll get it," said Flossie. She climbed onto the footstool and picked up the wall phone. "Hello," she said into the receiver.

"Flossie?" asked a frightened little voice. "This is Casey."

"What's wrong?" asked Flossie.

"I'm at the bakery," Casey said. "That crazy cake crook came back! And this time he didn't steal just a cake!"

3

A Three-Layer
Crime

"What did he steal?" Flossie exclaimed. Bert, Nan, and Freddie quickly gathered around her, trying to hear what Casey was saying.

Flossie's friend sounded very upset. "I just found out—early this afternoon he stole our delivery list! It had the names and addresses of everyone we delivered to today."

"How does she know it was the same man?" Bert asked, and Flossie repeated the question to Casey.

"One of the workers saw him run out the back door," Casey said nervously. "A short man wearing a trench coat and a hooded mask." Casey was silent for a moment. Then she said softly, "Why does he keep stealing from us, Flossie? I'm scared."

"Don't worry," said Flossie. "We'll do everything we can to help you."

The other Bobbseys moved away while Flossie tried to calm her friend.

"I feel like we're in a bad TV comedy," said Nan. "There's actually somebody out there stealing *cakes!*"

"He's not just stealing them," Bert added. "He's smashing them. And he's taking a lot of risks just to do it. Why?"

"Maybe it's somebody who doesn't like cake," Freddie offered.

"Nah," said Bert. "So far, this guy is only stealing Baker's Bakery cakes."

"Maybe it's somebody with a grudge against the Bakers," said Nan.

"Who has a grudge against the Bakers?" asked Mrs. Bobbsey as she entered the kitchen.

Nan, Bert, and Freddie quickly filled her in on the latest theft at the bakery.

"That is strange," said Mrs. Bobbsey. "But it could be someone's idea of a joke."

"I don't think so, Mom." Nan leaned against the kitchen counter and scratched her head. "I don't get it—cakes aren't valuable, like money or jewelry."

"Well, I'll figure it all out later," said Bert. He headed toward the refrigerator. "Right now I need some brain food to help me think."

Nan chuckled. "There's not that much food in the country," she said.

"Very funny," said Bert. "Now, what's to eat?"

"Don't spoil your appetite," said Mrs. Bobbsey. "Mrs. Green has a meat loaf in the oven. We'll be having dinner soon."

Bert, Nan, and Freddie let out a low moan. They all liked Mrs. Green, but they didn't like her cooking. Her meat loaf was tough, her gravy was watery, and she served creamed spinach with every meal.

"Never mind," said Mrs. Bobbsey, smiling. "Just don't touch that chocolate cake in there."

Bert looked inside the refrigerator. Then he turned to his mother with a puzzled look on his face. "What chocolate cake? There's no cake in here."

Freddie ran to the refrigerator and looked inside. The cake was gone. "Oh, no!" he shouted. "Not again!"

A few minutes later the kitchen was buzzing with excitement. All four twins, Mrs. Bobbsey, and Mrs. Green were busily searching the room for clues. Even Chief was sniffing around for the missing cake.

"But I put it in there myself," said Mrs. Green. "Right after the delivery man left."

"Well, I didn't take it," said Freddie. "I was

with Mom the whole time." He looked at Flossie.

"I didn't touch it!" Flossie exclaimed. "I went into the living room and fell asleep watching TV. Ask Chief, he was sleeping right next to me."

"On my couch?" asked Mrs. Bobbsey with a groan.

Chief let out a little whine.

"He was guarding me, Mom." Flossie reached down and scratched Chief's ear.

"Some guard dog," said Mrs. Bobbsey.

Suddenly Nan yelled, "Look at this!" She pointed to some dark smudges on the windowsill.

Everyone dashed over.

"How did that dirt get there?" asked Mrs. Green. "I cleaned this room early this afternoon."

"It's not dirt," Nan said. "It's mud."

Bert pulled out his Rex Sleuther Pocket Crime-Solver. Rex was Bert's favorite storybook detective. The Crime-Solver was shaped like a large Swiss army knife and contained a number of handy gadgets.

Bert extracted the magnifying glass and examined the smears. "It's mud, all right—a muddy footprint, leading *into* the house."

"A burglar!" Mrs. Green said with alarm.

"Calm down, Mrs. Green." Although Mrs. Bobbsey was controlling herself, she was upset, too. "We don't have all the facts yet."

"I bet whoever it was stepped in Mom's flower bed outside," said Freddie. "Maybe they left another footprint. Come on, Flossie."

Freddie and Flossie grabbed a flashlight and their coats, and dashed outside. As they left, Bert dropped to his knees. He began crawling toward the refrigerator, carefully searching the floor with his magnifying glass. Thinking Bert was playing, Chief kept trying to lick his face and push him over.

"Not now, Chief," said Bert, dodging another of the pet's sloppy kisses. He had to push the dog away gently several times before he reached a spot in front of the refrigerator. "The thief definitely headed straight for the cake. There are little smears of dried mud leading right up to the fridge."

Nan turned toward the housekeeper. "What time did you clean the kitchen, Mrs. Green?"

Mrs. Green put a finger to her lips. "About one-thirty."

"Was that before or after the cake was delivered?" asked Nan.

Mrs. Green thought for a moment. "Why— it was after."

"I wonder why Chief didn't bark when the

thief came in." Bert looked at the friendly sheepdog sitting next to him.

"Oh, my!" Mrs. Green exclaimed. "While I was cleaning the living room, he kept chasing the vacuum-cleaner hose. So I put him in the den and closed the door." The housekeeper lowered her head. "He started barking soon after, but I thought he just wanted to get out. I'm so sorry, Mrs. Bobbsey."

"That's all right," said Mrs. Bobbsey. "How could you have known?"

"Mom," said Bert, "Nan and I are going to check this room for more clues. Maybe you and Mrs. Green should see if anything else is missing."

"That's a good idea," Mrs. Bobbsey said, turning to march toward the door. "We'll start with the bedrooms upstairs."

As Mrs. Green followed their mother from the room, Bert and Nan began carefully searching the kitchen.

Out in the backyard, Freddie and Flossie were following a very clear trail. The trail led from the flower bed, across the backyard, and toward the garage.

As they neared the front of the garage, Flossie grabbed her brother's arm. "Be careful, Freddie. He might still be around here."

"I doubt it," said Freddie. "It's been raining off and on since this morning. The Cakenapper wouldn't be dumb enough to stand around in the rain all day."

Freddie sounded confident. But it was getting dark, and there were spooky shadows all around the yard. As they came around the far side of the building, Freddie moved very slowly and carefully.

When Flossie and he turned the corner, they stopped short.

"Do you see what I see?" Freddie asked with excitement. He aimed the flashlight at something on the ground.

"I sure do," said Flossie, nodding her head. "Let's tell the others, fast."

The two children quickly turned and raced back to the house.

Bert and Nan had just finished searching the kitchen when Freddie and Flossie burst in.

"I was right!" Freddie shouted. "Someone did come across the lawn. He walked right through Mom's flower bed."

"And he left the same way," Flossie added. "We followed his footprints to the garage. And then we found—"

"The cake!" Freddie interrupted.

"It was all mashed up behind the garage,"

Flossie continued. "The thief must have dropped it when he ran away."

"Or he smashed it up—just like the one in the diner," Nan said. She looked thoughtful. "Maybe he smashed the one he stole from the bakery, too."

Flossie ran over to the telephone. "I'm going to call Casey. I want to find out if any other cakes have been smashed."

"I want to know why he stole the Bakers' delivery list," said Freddie. He slid down to the floor and sat next to Chief.

"None of this makes any sense," said Bert. "This crook steals three cakes in the same day. As far as we know, he smashes two of them. And he steals the bakery's delivery list—*after* they'd already made the deliveries."

Nan rested her chin in her hands and sighed. "You're right. This *doesn't* make any sense."

Just then Mrs. Bobbsey and Mrs. Green returned to the kitchen.

"So far, nothing else is missing," said Mrs. Bobbsey. She leaned against the counter and folded her arms.

"Then it looks like all he stole was the chocolate cake," said Nan.

"Maybe we should call the police," suggested Mrs. Green.

"We most certainly should," said Mrs. Bobbsey. There was an angry tone in her voice.

Bert could tell his mother was upset, so he tried to cheer her up. "What would they arrest him for?" he asked with a slight smile. "Cake mushing? That charge wouldn't . . . stick."

Though everyone groaned at Bert's joke, Mrs. Bobbsey knew he was trying to make her feel better. She gave Bert a quick hug, and then she and Mrs. Green went out to check the damage to the flower bed.

"I think we'd better start investigating," Nan said seriously.

"Yeah," Bert agreed. "This guy is up to something, and he's moving pretty fast. Tomorrow's Saturday. Nan and I have to be at Bradley Allnut's party by noon. So we'll start investigating first thing in the morning."

"And since all this started at Baker's Bakery, let's go there first," said Nan. "This crook might be after the Bakers."

"Then it's up to us to stop him," Flossie declared.

"That's right," said Bert. He waved his Rex Sleuther Crime-Solver over his head like a sword. "Beware, Cakenapper! The Bobbseys are on the case."

4

Recipe for a Suspect

On Saturday morning the sun was barely shining through the clouds as the Bobbseys arrived at Baker's Bakery. The autumn air was cold, and the wind sent the leaves swirling along the quiet streets.

The Bobbseys chained their bikes to a pole, then hurried through the front door.

Inside, customers sat at the tables, eating delicious-looking pastries. Freddie and Flossie couldn't stop staring as they walked by.

At first the Bobbseys didn't see anyone behind the counter. But as they got closer, Mr. Baker appeared from the kitchen.

"Good morning," he said cheerfully when he saw Flossie. "I'm afraid Casey isn't here yet."

Flossie introduced the other twins, and then Nan told him about their suspicions.

"I know it's not much to go on," she concluded. "But it looks like someone is *really* out to get you."

"I find all this hard to believe." Mr. Baker seemed puzzled. "We don't have any enemies. Unless . . ."

Nan moved closer. "Unless what, sir?"

"Well, there's Lew Sugarman," Mr. Baker said. "He's a high-school student who used to work for us. He handled supplies and helped make deliveries. Then he got into a fight with another worker. So we fired him about a month ago. He vowed he'd get even, but I didn't take him seriously."

"That sounds like our man," Freddie said to his brother.

"We don't know that yet," Bert said. "Sleuther's rule number ten: Never jump to conclusions." Bert was always quoting from his Rex Sleuther manual.

"Can you think of anybody else?" asked Nan. She took out a small pad and pencil and wrote down Lew's name.

"This will sound silly." Mr. Baker ran his fingers through his thinning hair. "But there is Egbert Farley."

"Who is Egbert Farley?" asked Flossie.

"He's a health-food nut," Mr. Baker replied. "Egbert is the head of a small group called P.A.C., People Against Chocolate."

"Oh, I've seen him," said Nan. "He's always making speeches in front of candy stores and stuff. And he hands out buttons that say 'Be a Choc-Stopper.'"

"That's him," Mr. Baker said with a nod. "When we moved in here, Egbert's little group marched in front of our store for days. He said that sooner or later he'd show people how bad chocolate really is."

"Well, too much sweet stuff isn't good for you," admitted Nan sheepishly.

"I don't know about that," said Flossie. She was watching a customer eat a huge piece of banana cream pie. "That couldn't possibly be bad for me."

Bert chuckled, then turned to Nan. "You sound just like Mom."

"Your sister's right, Bert. You shouldn't eat too many sweets. But I think Egbert is going a little too far."

"Are those the only people you can think of?" asked Nan.

"That's it," Mr. Baker said, shrugging his shoulders. "But I can't imagine either of them stealing a cake or a delivery list."

"The delivery list!" Bert suddenly snapped

his fingers. "That reminds me. Do you have a copy of that list?"

"I'm afraid not," Mr. Baker replied. "They were mostly phone orders. We wrote them down on our delivery sheet and then gave it to the driver."

"How about your sales receipts?" asked Nan. "Couldn't you look at copies of the receipts and see who you delivered to yesterday?"

Mr. Baker shook his head. "The receipts were clipped to the delivery list."

"Have you heard about any other cakenappings?" asked Freddie. He was talking to Mr. Baker, but his eyes were fixed on a platter of cookies topped with raspberry jam.

"No, I haven't," Mr. Baker replied. "If Sugarman or Farley is responsible, I'll be very surprised."

"I think we should ask them some questions," said Flossie. She watched the banana-cream-pie customer pop the last piece into his mouth.

"Right," Freddie added, looking up from the cookies. "Do you know where they live?"

Mr. Baker gave the Bobbseys Lew Sugarman's address, but he didn't know where Egbert Farley lived.

The twins decided they could get the address

from the phone book. They thanked Mr. Baker, said goodbye, and headed home.

As the twins approached their house, they were surprised to see a police car parked right in front of it. They recognized the officer standing at their back door as Sergeant Molly Franklin. The sergeant kept checking a sheet of paper as she talked to Mrs. Bobbsey.

"Hi, Sergeant Franklin," said Bert as he got off his bike. "Are you here about the Cakenapper?"

The police officer smiled. "I'm here about the *break-in*. I'm checking the information the officers took from you yesterday evening."

"Do you think you'll catch him?" asked Flossie.

Sergeant Franklin looked down into Flossie's big blue eyes. "Honestly, Flossie—I don't know. We've all been pretty busy trying to catch this North Side burglar. Catching a cake thief—well, that might take a little more time."

"Okay," said Freddie. "As soon as we catch this cakenapper, we'll help you catch that burglar."

Sergeant Franklin smiled. "Freddie, as Lieutenant Pike always says—"

"Leave police work to the police," the twins interrupted in unison.

"Right," said Sergeant Franklin. She finished checking the report, said goodbye, and drove off in her police car.

"Are you two going to be on time for Bradley's party?" said Mrs. Bobbsey, looking at Bert and Nan.

"The party doesn't start for another two hours, Mom," Bert replied. "We've got plenty of time."

"I hope so," said Mrs. Bobbsey. She turned and went into the house.

"Now we know for sure," Nan said to the other Bobbseys. "The police aren't going to put these cake thefts at the top of their list—not with the North Side burglar stealing money and jewels."

"That definitely makes this our case," said Bert. "So, let's go inside and look up Mr. Farley."

It took them a few minutes to find Egbert Farley's address in the directory.

"I know that neighborhood," said Nan. "I'll go see Mr. Farley."

"That leaves me with Lew Sugarman," said Bert. He looked a little worried. "And he doesn't live in a great part of town. Not great at all."

Freddie and Flossie came up with their own assignment. They volunteered to ride around the neighborhood to look for more victims of the Cakenapper.

Flossie smiled. "Even if we don't find the Cakenapper, we might find some cake."

One hour later, Bert arrived in Lew Sugarman's neighborhood.

The houses were old and run-down. Their paint was peeling, and the porches sagged. Even the mailboxes needed repairs.

Bert felt uneasy. He noticed a number of older kids hanging out on the streets. They were watching him closely—and their looks weren't friendly.

The Sugarmans' house was at the end of a dead-end street. The railroad yard was just beyond, behind a rusted wire fence to keep people out. Bert noticed that a large hole had been cut in the fence.

I guess the kids go in there to play, thought Bert. He rode his bike up the Sugarmans' driveway to the backyard.

There he saw a muscular teenage boy working with a wrench on an old car. Bert noticed that it was a dark color—just like the car Freddie had seen leaving the diner!

Bert took a few steps toward the boy. "Excuse me," he said. "Are you Lew Sugarman?"

The boy looked up from under the hood. He

seemed as tough and unfriendly as the kids Bert had passed on the street.

"Yeah," said the teenager. He glared at Bert. "I'm Lew. So what?"

Bert cleared his throat and tried to sound confident. "I'm Bert Bobbsey. I'd like to talk to you about Baker's Bakery."

Lew suddenly stood up straight and threw his wrench on the ground. "Who are you—the new errand boy? Did Mr. Baker send you here to hassle me?"

"No, I'm not the errand boy," Bert said strongly. "I'm here to find out who's hassling the Bakers. Somebody's been smashing their cakes all over town. He's even stolen from the bakery."

"And you think I'm the one?" Lew's eyes went cold. "Well, if I am, Errand Boy—you've made a bad mistake." An evil grin appeared on Lew's face. He began pounding his fist into the palm of his other hand as he moved toward Bert. "It was pretty stupid, coming here alone."

Bert tensed. He knew Lew was right. Coming alone had been a mistake—possibly the biggest mistake he'd ever made.

5

Warnings by the Dozen

Bert held his ground as Lew walked up to him slowly. He never took his eyes away from the older boy's, even though he knew that at any second Lew might take a swing at him.

"You don't scare easy, do you?" Lew asked with a challenge in his voice.

"I scare easy," Bert said evenly. "I just don't run."

Lew looked at Bert for a moment. Then he burst out laughing. "You're okay, kid." Lew gave Bert a friendly wallop on the shoulder. The force nearly knocked Bert over. "You've got guts."

"Thanks," said Bert. He tried to rub his sore shoulder without Lew noticing.

Lew continued chuckling as he turned and walked back to his car. "Look, uh, er . . ."

"Bert."

"Look, Bert," Lew continued. "Mr. Baker and I had a few arguments, but nothing worth smashing his stuff for."

"Didn't you say you'd get even with him when he fired you?" Bert asked.

"Sure I did," Lew said. Slowly a look of sadness came over his face. "I was mad. I needed that job. Things have been kind of tough for my folks, and I—I—"

"I get it," said Bert.

"I've had trouble finding work since I lost that job," Lew admitted. "I have a bad temper, you know."

"Who, you? Nah," Bert teased. He saw a slight grin appear on Lew's face. "So . . . you're not the guy."

"No," Lew said truthfully. "I need to get another delivery job. But first I have to get my car to work. It hasn't run for a week."

Bert realized he was on the wrong trail. If Lew's car didn't work, he couldn't be the guy who'd driven away from the diner. Besides, Freddie and Flossie had said the cake smasher was short. Lew Sugarman was anything but short.

Lew might have been angry at the Bakers a

month ago, Bert thought, but he wasn't now. That was certain.

"Well, I'd better go," said Bert.

"Okay, kid. Take it easy." Lew still looked a little sad as he stared at his car.

Bert mounted his bike and started to pedal away, then stopped. "Did you ever think of asking Mr. Baker for your job back?"

Lew looked up in surprise.

"He's not a bad guy," Bert said with a smile.

Lew smiled back.

Five minutes later Bert was almost out of Lew's part of town. He looked around and saw the same kids still hanging out on the streets. But this time a few of them didn't look half as mean.

Bert remembered telling Freddie about Sleuther rule number ten: Never jump to conclusions. He'd have to keep it in mind, too.

Nan Bobbsey hadn't found Egbert Farley at home, but a neighbor had told her where he worked. Mr. Farley was part owner of a health-food store called Vitamin Delicious.

When Nan arrived at the store, Mr. Farley was more than happy to talk to her. As a matter of fact, he hadn't stopped talking since she'd walked through the door.

"Mr. Farley, I—"

"Natural energy, that's what we're talking about here!" said the thin, middle-aged man. He pointed to a chart behind the counter. It was a complete list of natural foods and the vitamins in them. "Aside from your basic fruits, there are hundreds of other ways to give the body energy! Who needs candy?"

"I know about—" Nan tried to say.

"Rice polish. That's the outer covering of brown rice. It's chock-full of vitamin B and minerals." Mr. Farley was speaking very fast. His eyes sparkled with excitement.

"Then there's wheat germ. Now, that contains vitamin E, which is good for healing skin problems. Very good."

"Mr. Farley," Nan said quickly, "I didn't come to buy anything. I really came to ask you about Baker's Bakery. They're—"

"A hazard to your health," he interrupted. "They use the very things I warn people against. Processed sugar, chemicals, food coloring, and—"

"Excuse me, sir!" It was Nan's turn to interrupt. "Mr. and Mrs. Baker use a lot of natural products in their baked goods. That's why so many people like them."

"They don't use dried seaweed instead of regular salt, do they?"

"Well—"

"They don't use millet as a natural food coloring for their cakes," Mr. Farley continued.

"Not everyone likes—"

"And they don't use carob instead of chocolate! Do they?"

"No," Nan replied hotly. "They don't use all those things. But that's no reason to steal and smash their cakes."

Egbert Farley suddenly looked very confused. "What are you talking about?"

Nan quickly explained.

"And you thought that I would— Oh, my." He began drumming his long, thin fingers on the countertop. "That *is* terrible. I march in front of candy stores, and I make signs and buttons. But I would never steal. And I would never destroy. Oh, I hope the Bakers don't think— Oh, my."

Nan was surprised. For the first time since she'd arrived, Mr. Farley was speechless. He just stood there, looking very upset.

"Don't worry, Mr. Farley," Nan said. Suddenly she wanted to make him feel better. "Mr. and Mrs. Baker don't think you're responsible. Honest. They, uh . . . hoped you might know something that could help us find the crook."

It worked. The store owner became very excited. He promised he'd keep an eye out for any suspicious-looking characters. And he'd report anything he uncovered to the Bakers.

As Nan headed for the door, Mr. Farley called out, "Don't worry, young lady. We'll catch this scoundrel."

"I hope you're right," said Nan.

"I am," said Mr. Farley. "By the way, I'm about to have lunch. A great big bowl of yogurt with wheat germ and raw honey. Would you like some?"

"No, thank you," Nan replied. "I'm going to a friend's party. I'll eat there."

"I hope the food will be good and healthy," Mr. Farley said eagerly.

Nan thought about all the ice cream and cake there would be at Bradley's party. Maybe it won't be healthy, she thought, but it sure will be *good*. She waved goodbye to Egbert Farley and left the store.

On the ride to Bradley Allnut's house, Nan tried to add up the clues the twins had so far. She quickly realized that they didn't know very much. The Cakenapper had struck in three places, yet nobody knew what he really looked like since he had worn a mask. But Freddie, Flossie, and Mrs. Bobbsey all had described him as being short.

Nan decided she needed to visit the scene of

the first crime again. Maybe the cake thief had left some clue that no one had found yet. So she made a detour and rode over to Baker's Bakery.

Nan didn't go inside when she arrived. Instead, she chained her bike to a lamppost, then walked up and down the block. She looked around very carefully.

Her path took her alongside the shop and to the alley in back. Nothing.

Nan returned to the main street. One by one she peered in the windows of the stores that were near the bakery. Again, nothing.

Finally Nan decided to go across the street to the bus depot. It would have been a perfect place for the cakenapper to hide after he stole the first cake.

Nan entered the large and busy one-story building. To her left was a row of windows. In front of each window was a line of people waiting to buy tickets. In the center of the big room was a group of benches for people to sit on. And on her right, down a narrow hallway, there was a small room with pay lockers where travelers could leave their bags. The sign said it cost twenty-five cents.

There are people everywhere, Nan thought. If one of them is the Cakenapper, how will I know?

Nan continued looking around the station but finally left without any new clues.

There must be something we're missing, Nan thought as she walked back to her bike. Something small but important that could pull this whole crazy case together. Something that would tell us we're on the right track.

That something was waiting for her when she reached her bike.

In the carry basket was a carton of eggs. When Nan lifted the lid she saw that every single egg had been cracked open. A gooey mess had already begun to leak from the carton. It dripped and oozed along the frame of her bike and down the rear tire.

Then Nan saw the note. It was written on the underside of the lid. Nan read it, and her eyes widened. The message was brief but clear.

"Stay out of my business," the note said. "Or you'll find out something—eggs aren't the only things that break."

6

A Birthday Surprise

Nan looked around quickly, hoping to spot somebody suspicious. But everyone she saw seemed to be acting normally.

Nan could feel her anger growing. This isn't silly anymore, she thought. The Cakenapper has scared my sister, broken into our house, and now he's threatening me.

Nan quickly threw the broken eggs into a trash can. She pulled a tissue from her pocket and cleaned off the carton. "Evidence for the police handwriting expert," she said softly as she dropped the carton into her bike basket.

After cleaning the goo from her bike, Nan hopped on and headed for Bradley's party.

"Okay, Cakenapper," said Nan. "I hope you have a lot more eggs. Because the Bobbseys are going to scramble them, but good."

The party was in full swing when Nan arrived. She put Bradley's present on a table with all the others, then looked around. Red and white Happy Birthday streamers were tacked over the doorways and draped over the windows. Balloons dangled from strings taped to the ceiling.

Bradley's mother had set up party games in three of the downstairs rooms. There were dart games, ring-tossing games, and even indoor basketball.

But the living room had the best games of all. Two TV sets were placed a few feet apart. Attached to each one was a great video game.

Nan was amazed. Everywhere she looked there were games to play—only no one was playing them. They couldn't. Mrs. Allnut had the kids lined up as if they were going into school. She was treating them as if they were a bunch of five-year-olds.

"Hey," said a whiny voice. "I was first."

"Not anymore," came a nasty reply. "Want to make something of it?"

Nan recognized the second voice instantly. It belonged to Danny Rugg. She looked toward the head of the dart game line, and there he was, pushing ahead of everyone.

Danny was a first-class rat—the school bully. The Bobbseys had crossed his path before, and they always outsmarted him. But that didn't make him any easier to be around. In fact, it made him even more of a colossal pain.

"Hi, Nan," came a nervous little voice from behind her. "Glad you could make my party."

It was Bradley Allnut. He was a chubby boy with light brown hair and big eyes. He was the only kid wearing a suit. His tie was crooked.

"Hi, Brad," said Nan. "It looks like it's going to be another great party."

Bradley lowered his head. "I want it to be fun," he said, "but Mom won't let us do anything. She's got the kids lining up so she can hand out game stuff."

"She always does that," Nan said. "But don't worry. We always have a good time."

Bradley looked up and grinned. "You bet we will," he said. He took a quick step backward and stumbled over someone's foot.

Nan turned away quickly so Bradley wouldn't be too embarrassed. She spotted Bert coming out of the kitchen carrying a soda, and walked over to him.

"How long have you been here?" Nan asked.

"Too long," Bert said dryly. "I had a short

visit with Lew Sugarman. It didn't take me long to figure out he's not our man."

Bert quickly gave Nan the details.

"I didn't do much better with Mr. Farley. But . . ." Nan told Bert about the warning. "Whoever left it must have spotted me after I reached Baker's Bakery."

"Maybe not," said Bert. "It's possible that Mr. Farley followed you to the bakery. He could have waited until you went into the bus station, then planted the message."

"Maybe," said Nan. "But I don't think so. Are you sure it isn't Lew Sugarman?"

"Yep," said Bert. He leaned back against the wall. "I don't think smashing cakes is at the top of his list of things to do."

Nan watched Mrs. Allnut handing out rubber darts, little plastic basketballs, and other party favors. Bradley's mother was very careful to make sure she had enough for everybody.

"So where does that leave us?" Nan asked with a sigh.

"Nowhere," said Bert. "This case sure isn't a *piece of cake.*" Bert smiled. Nan didn't.

Just then Mrs. Allnut handed a plastic basketball to Bert and some darts to Nan. Then she walked to the center of the room and stood next to Bradley.

Poor Brad, thought Nan. He looks really embarrassed.

"Now, children," Mrs. Allnut said cheerfully. "I've made sure each of you has a party favor. Let's see them." All the children moaned and held up their party favors. "That means all of you will be able to play these darling little games. So—in a calm and orderly fashion, let us walk to the game of our choice."

Those were the magic words.

Everyone broke out of line and ran yelling and screaming through the house. They pushed and shoved and argued to get to the games. They left trails of party snacks along the hallways, spilled drinks, and accidentally broke two flower vases.

Mrs. Allnut did her best to control the situation. But finally she just shook her head and smiled.

This always happens at Brad's parties, thought Nan and Bert as they played games and sampled the food. It was the main reason everybody came. It was fun.

An hour later, Mrs. Allnut walked into the living room with a huge chocolate birthday cake. It was four layers high and sprinkled with crushed walnuts. Carefully arranged on top was a beautiful ring of sliced cherries. *Happy*

Birthday, Bradley was written in the center in glistening red icing.

"One of Baker's Bakery's special birthday cakes," said Mrs. Allnut with a big smile.

Bert and Nan were among the first to be served. They were moving away from the table as Danny Rugg pushed his way to the front.

"Why don't you wait your turn, Danny?" said Nan. "There's plenty for everybody."

"Because I want to get a big piece before they run out," Danny said, sneering. "I just want to get mine."

Nan shook her head and walked away with Bert. "I hope he gets *his,* all right."

"Don't worry," said Bert. "He will."

They sat down on a couple of empty chairs near a sliding glass door. The door looked out onto the patio. "Boy, this cake sure looks good," said Bert. "I—"

"Aaaaaagh!"

The scream ripped through the room and stopped everything. Half the children froze where they stood. No one knew what was going on. But Bert and Nan spotted the source of the trouble and ran right to it—Danny Rugg. Danny was holding his jaw with one hand, and in his other hand he held—

"A key!" Danny yelled. "I bit down on a key!

Somebody put a key in my cake. You won't get away with this."

Mrs. Allnut, Bradley, and a few of the kids rushed to Danny's side.

"Oh, I'm so sorry," said Mrs. Allnut.

"I hope it doesn't hurt—much," said Bradley, trying not to smile.

Danny noticed that everyone was looking at him. "Uh, yeah, yeah. It hurts," he whined. "Oh, it hurts awful."

"Danny isn't really in pain," Bert whispered to Nan. "He keeps holding different places on his face. He's faking it just to get attention."

"That figures." Nan sounded annoyed.

Nan turned and walked away. She decided that Danny Rugg wasn't going to ruin this party for her. There was still a big piece of chocolate cake she hadn't finished.

Nan reached her chair and picked up her plate. She speared a piece of cake on her fork and raised it to her lips. But just as she was about to put it in her mouth, her gaze fell on the sliding glass door. On the other side, staring in at her, was a man with blazing eyes. Blazing eyes—and wearing a black hood.

"Bert," Nan yelled. "He's here! The Cakenapper is here!"

7

The Chocolate-covered Clue

At the sound of Nan's warning to Bert, the masked man took off.

Nan quickly put her plate down and pulled open the sliding door. As she raced outside, Bert came up beside her.

"Did you see him?" Nan asked as they ran alongside the house.

"No," Bert said. "And I don't think anyone else did, either. He moved too fast."

The twins rounded the corner and found themselves standing in the Allnuts' crowded driveway. Two cars and a catering truck took up most of the space.

Suddenly Bert and Nan spotted a dark car speeding away from the house.

"Come on," Bert shouted. "Maybe we can get his license plate number."

But by the time they reached the road, the car had disappeared over the hill.

"Terrific," Bert said in disgust. "Our big chance—and we lose him."

"Well," said Nan, "at least he didn't smash this cake."

"Yeah," said Bert. "But this guy's as fast as the North Side burglar. He stole three cakes in one day."

"I wish we knew how many cakes the Bakers delivered yesterday," Nan said thoughtfully. "And how many they baked."

Bert nodded. "That might help. Let's talk to Flossie when we get home."

As they walked back to Bradley's house, a van pulled up and four adults got out. They were dressed in the silliest animal costumes the Bobbseys had ever seen.

"Excuse me," said the man dressed like a skunk. "Is this little Bradley Allnut's party? We're the Fuzzy Buddy Players, and we're here to help you kids have fun."

Bert and Nan lowered their heads and softly mumbled, "Oh, terrific." They led the skunk and his friends inside.

* * *

Late that afternoon, the twins gathered in Freddie's room. Bert was pacing back and forth, while Nan sat on the bed, sketching. Freddie was at his computer, nibbling on a candy bar. Flossie was on the floor with Chief.

"Okay," said Bert. "We've told Freddie everything we know about the Cakenapper. He's put all of it into his computer, including what happened at Brad's party."

"What does it add up to?" Nan asked.

Freddie finished his candy bar and threw the foil into his trash basket. He punched a series of buttons. The computer beeped and a list appeared on the screen.

"Not much," said Freddie with a shake of his head. "He's stolen or smashed three of Baker's cakes, so far. He drives a dark car. He wears a black hood over his face."

"And we know he's mean." Nan poked at the smelly egg carton. "Only someone really mean would leave a message like this."

"Maybe it's somebody who doesn't like the Bakers," said Flossie. She was trying to keep Chief from sticking his head in Freddie's trash basket. The shaggy dog seemed to be looking for something.

"You two rode all over the neighborhood," said Nan. "Did you find any more cake theft victims?"

"Not exactly . . ." Flossie ducked her head so Nan couldn't see her face.

"We didn't actually ride *all* over the neighborhood . . ." said Freddie.

"What do you mean?" asked Bert. He could tell that the younger twins were hiding something.

Flossie put on one of her sweetest smiles. "We sort of got stuck at Mrs. DiAngelo's. She makes the best peanut-butter fudge."

"Flossie got most of the fudge," Freddie declared. "I only got—"

"Never mind," said Nan. "We get the message."

"I wish we had a few Double-Double Chocolate Chunkies," said Flossie. Again she had to pull their dog away from the wastebasket. "Chocolate always helps me think."

"Chocolate . . ." Bert suddenly stopped pacing. "Freddie, punch up everything Flossie told us about that first cake theft at the bakery."

Again Freddie's fingers hit a few keys. A second later, Flossie's statement appeared on the screen.

Bert read it carefully, then smiled. "Just what I thought. Floss, you said they were making a batch of cakes, right?"

Flossie sat up quickly. "Sure. Twelve—I think."

"Were all of them chocolate?" Bert asked eagerly.

Flossie thought for a moment. "No. There was angel food—and carrot."

Suddenly Nan caught on. "But the Cakenapper only smashes chocolate cakes. No carrot cakes and no angel food."

"Great!" Freddie exclaimed as he typed in the new information. "But what does it mean?"

For a minute everyone was silent. Then Chief made another lunge for the trash can. "Stop it, Chief," Flossie said sternly. "Why do you want to play with Freddie's wastebasket, anyway?"

"He doesn't want the basket," said Freddie. "He wants the candy wrapper I threw inside."

Nan looked at Freddie, Chief, and the wastebasket, and then snapped her fingers. "Inside!" she shouted. "He wanted something inside!"

Bert looked at Nan, and the two of them shouted together, "He wanted the key inside the cake!"

Freddie and Flossie cheered, and Chief began to bark.

"Great," said Flossie, rubbing her hands together. "I just have one question. Why does he want the key?"

"Uh . . ." Nan looked a little confused. "Good question."

"We'll find the answer," said Bert, "as soon as we examine the key."

"Where *is* the key?" Freddie asked.

"Danny Rugg still has it," Nan said.

"Oh, great," said Freddie, rolling his eyes.

"He said something about showing it to his mother," Nan said.

"Well, that key might be important evidence," said Bert. "And we need it more than Danny does. Maybe I'd better go—"

"Let Freddie and me handle it," Nan said. "We'll get the key somehow."

"Good," said Bert. "Because that means I can take Flossie with me—to the police station. I want to tell Lieutenant Pike what we've discovered. Maybe he can think of something that will help us."

Nan smiled and added, "And he's always willing to talk to Flossie."

"Right," said Bert, grinning. "Look, it's almost five o'clock now. We can do all this and be back in time for dinner. So let's get going."

Nan and Freddie pedaled fast as they neared Danny's block. They were glad it was a short ride. The air was getting chilly, and the trees along Maplewood Avenue didn't block the strong wind.

Nan was shivering as they walked their bikes

up to Danny's front door. "This is real crummy weather," she said.

Freddie chuckled. "Crummy weather to visit a crummy guy." He pressed the doorbell.

"Well," Danny said when he answered the door. "If it isn't Nan and her little brother, *Fraidie.*"

Nan ignored Danny's dumb joke, but Freddie couldn't. "I'll show you who's afraid," he said angrily.

Nan grabbed his arm. "Wait a minute, Freddie. That's not why we came here." She turned to Danny. "Look, it's really important. Can we come in? It's about the key—the one you found in your piece of birthday cake."

"What about it?" Danny asked suspiciously.

"It's more valuable than you think. Can we talk about it, or not?"

Danny thought for a moment. Then he let them in.

Nan spent fifteen minutes trying to convince Danny to give them the key. She told him all about the smashed cakes, the break-ins, and the hooded Cakenapper. But no matter what she said, Danny just didn't want to believe her.

"You must think I'm pretty stupid," he said, glaring at them from a big easy chair.

"You're half right," Freddie mumbled.

Danny jumped up from the chair. "Why, you—" he shouted.

Nan stepped in between Danny and her brother. "Look, Danny. I'm telling you the truth."

"Sure, you are," said Danny nastily. "But I'm keeping this key until my folks get home. Then I'm going to tell them how Allnut tried to break my tooth."

"Danny," Nan pleaded, "this has nothing to do with—"

Just then the Ruggs' telephone rang.

"No deal," said Danny as he picked up the phone. "There's no way I'm giving you this key." He turned and spoke into the receiver. "Hello."

Nan and Freddie watched as Danny's smug expression suddenly changed. His eyes became very big, and his mouth dropped open.

Nan saw a look of fear appear on Danny's face. She quickly grabbed the phone and put it to her ear.

"I'll repeat it, kid," said a deep, gruff voice. "Put the key in an envelope and leave it in your mailbox. You have ten minutes. Do it—or else."

With a click, the phone went dead.

8
Too Many Crooks

"Here!" Danny exclaimed as Nan put down the phone. "Take your dumb old key! I don't want it anymore." He pulled the key out of his pocket and handed it to Nan.

Nan took the key from Danny and quickly looked it over. The handle was the size of a half-dollar, with a hole in it. The stem was the shape and size of a small pencil eraser.

"Let me see it," said Freddie. "Hey, there are some numbers carved in the metal. What do they mean?"

"I don't know yet," his sister said. Nan was puzzled. No matter how she looked at the key, she couldn't figure out what kind of lock it would fit.

Freddie was watching Danny. He'd never seen the older boy so nervous. "Changed your mind pretty fast," said Freddie.

"He had a good reason," said Nan. She quickly told Freddie about the creepy voice and the threat. "I don't blame Danny for being scared."

"Scared? Who's scared?" Danny tried to sound brave, but it wasn't working. "I'm—I'm just tired of looking at your faces. That's all."

"Oh," said Nan. She secretly winked at Freddie. "Then I guess we'd better go and leave you alone. *All* alone."

Nan and Freddie opened the front door.

"Hey, wait a minute," said Danny. He grabbed his coat and ran outside with the Bobbseys. "I was, uh . . . going over to my neighbor's house, anyway. I'll, uh, walk with you. Just to make sure nothing happens to you."

"Gee, thanks," Freddie mumbled as he and Nan headed for their bikes. "I feel safer already."

Bert and Flossie sat on a bench by the front desk of the Lakeport Police Department. The station was very busy.

Police officers jumped to answer the jangling phones. Others were checking the large map of

Lakeport that hung on a wall. Detectives were questioning people and taking notes. Other officers rushed out the door to follow up leads.

Bert and Flossie knew that some of the activity was just routine. But they could tell that most of it was connected to the North Side burglar. During the past twenty minutes they'd overheard lots of conversations about the clever thief.

"He's working fast. Six houses in six days."

"Clean as a whistle. No prints."

"That's right, Chief. We almost had him yesterday, but we blew it."

"We're doing everything we can, ma'am."

"Boy, the police really want to catch that crook," Flossie whispered to Bert. "That's why nobody has time to talk to us about our case."

"I know," Bert replied. "Even Lieutenant Pike is out there, searching."

Desk Sergeant Spooner looked up from his paperwork. "You kids are still here?"

"We sure are, Sergeant," said Bert. "We really need to see Lieutenant Pike."

The sergeant sighed. "I told you, Bert, the lieutenant is pretty busy right now. He could be gone for hours."

"Is he catching the burglar?" asked Flossie.

"He's trying, sweetheart, he's trying." Sergeant Spooner took a phone call, then turned

back to the kids. "Look, maybe I can help you. What's your problem?"

Bert and Flossie walked over to the police officer. Bert lifted Flossie onto the desk so she could see Sergeant Spooner.

For ten minutes the kids tried to explain about the Cakenapper. It was hard. The sergeant's phone kept ringing and people kept asking him questions. Finally, the Bobbseys finished telling their story.

The sergeant let out a deep sigh and rubbed his forehead.

"That's just what Lieutenant Pike does, whenever we help him solve a case," said Flossie. "Isn't it, Bert?"

"Uh, I'm sure he does," said the sergeant. "Look, I'll admit your cake smasher has been active. I've seen two reports about him myself. But this North Side crook has us all jumping. A lot of people are on our backs to get him."

"That must hurt," said Flossie.

Bert winced at his sister's joke, then turned to the officer. "Why are so many people pestering you?"

"Because some important people live in the North Side district," said the sergeant. "Mayor Childress, City Councilman Cox, and a few others."

"Wow!" Bert said in amazement. "You mean this crook robbed the mayor's house?"

"No, not at all," the sergeant said quickly. "But if we don't catch him soon— Well, who knows?"

"How does he break in?" Bert asked.

"We *think* he makes copies of the keys to the houses," said the sergeant. "But he may have picked the locks. If he did, he's good—a real professional crook."

"And he robbed six houses in six days?" asked Bert. He leaned in close to the police officer.

"Uh, yes," said the sergeant. "How'd—"

Flossie also closed in on the sergeant. "And you almost caught him yesterday, but you blew it."

"We lost him by the bus station," the sergeant admitted.

Bert's eyes lit up. "The bus station? You mean yesterday morning?"

"Yes." Sergeant Spooner started rubbing his forehead again. "We were chasing him from the scene of a crime, and we—"

"I bet that was the police car I saw near the bakery!" Flossie exclaimed.

"Right," said Bert. "Now I get it. Come on, Flossie." He helped Flossie down from the desk. "We've got to get home, fast. Thanks, Sergeant Spooner. You've been a lot of help."

"Wait a minute—"

"Yeah, thanks, Sergeant," said Flossie as she ran after Bert.

Outside, Bert grabbed his bike from the bike rack.

"Why are we rushing home?" asked Flossie as she reached her own bicycle.

"We're not, yet," Bert explained. "I want to use that pay phone on the corner."

When they reached the phone, Bert dropped in some coins and punched in a phone number.

Flossie was bursting with curiosity. "Who are you calling?"

"Danny Rugg," said Bert. "I'm trying to catch up with Nan and Freddie."

Bert let the phone ring for a long time, but no one answered.

"No good," he said as he hung up. "I hope they're on their way home."

Flossie became nervous. "Why are you so worried about them, Bert?"

"Because I think the North Side burglar has something to do with the Cakenapper," Bert said. "If I'm right, there's a dangerous crook after that key. And that means Nan, Freddie, and even Danny might be in real danger."

9
All the Ingredients

Bert and Flossie were relieved to find Nan and Freddie in the kitchen when they got home. Quickly Bert told them what they had learned at the police station.

"Well, Freddie and I weren't followed from Danny's," said Nan. "We kept checking."

"That's good," Bert said. "But it doesn't mean the crook won't be coming after the key sooner or later."

"Nan left a note in Danny's mailbox," Freddie said. "It told the Cakenapper that we were taking the key to the police."

"And we will," Flossie declared. "Just as soon as we figure out what it opens."

"So," Nan said, turning toward Bert. "You think the North Side burglar and the Cakenapper are the same person."

"They could be," said Bert. "Why else were they both around the bakery so early Friday morning?"

"That's right," said Freddie. "All this cake-smashing stuff started when Flossie went to visit the Bakers."

Nan was staring at the key Danny had given her. "I still can't figure out what kind of lock this key might fit."

"Let me have a look at it," Bert said. He took the key and turned it over a few times. "Maybe the numbers on it mean it's a bank key. You know, like a safe deposit box. But how would a bank key get into a cake?"

Just then, the phone rang.

Bert reached over and picked it up. He was happy to hear his mother's voice, but he was even more excited by the news she gave him.

"That was Mom," Bert said as he hung up the phone. "She said she's going to be late getting home. Guess why?"

Nan, Flossie, and Freddie all shrugged their shoulders.

"She's at police headquarters. There's been a break in the North Side robbery case."

"What kind of break?" Nan asked eagerly.

"The police think they know who the crook is—a guy named 'Fingers' Cranowsky. Mom says if they're right, Fingers is long gone. He only robs six places in the same town, then he takes off."

"If he's gone," said Flossie, "he can't be our Cakenapper."

Nan looked disappointed as she said, "You're right. You and Bert heard the police say that he's already hit six places. So why would he stick around here, chasing a key?"

"Yeah," said Freddie. "He'd be taking a big chance."

Bert grabbed his coat and headed for the back door. "I still have a hunch that Fingers and the Cakenapper connect somehow."

"And if they do?" asked Nan.

"Then we need to go back to the bakery. There's an old saying that the criminal always returns to the scene of the crime."

By the time the twins reached the bakery, it was drizzling. A few Saturday-evening shoppers were still inside. Mr. and Mrs. Baker, Casey, and a salesgirl were helping them.

Casey spotted the Bobbseys first. "Hi!" she called. She tugged at her mother's white apron. "Mom—look who's here."

Mr. Baker waved hello to the twins as Mrs.

Baker and Casey came from behind the counter.

"How are our junior detectives doing this evening?" asked Mrs. Baker. "Have you tracked down the cake thief?"

"We've almost got him," Flossie said proudly. "Nan and Bert think he's—"

"A rotten person for doing this to you," Nan interrupted. She quickly signaled Flossie not to say any more. "Uh, we need to check for more clues, Mrs. Baker. Would it be okay if we looked around the kitchen?"

"Could they, Mom?" Casey pleaded.

"Well," Mrs. Baker said slowly, "I guess it's all right. But the kitchen's a little messy. One of our helpers *was* cleaning up in there, but he had to make a rush delivery. Try not to get anything on yourselves."

"Thanks," said Nan.

"I'll go with them—in case they need help," said Casey. "Okay?"

"I guess we can spare you for a while," Mrs. Baker said. She winked at the children, then went back to helping customers.

The Bobbseys and Casey quickly ran into the back of the shop.

"Sorry, Floss," said Nan once they were in the kitchen. "I didn't want to say anything about Fingers until we were sure."

Bert gave Flossie a quick hug. "Okay, Flossie and Casey—show us exactly what happened yesterday morning."

The two girls told all about the cooking, the tour of the storeroom, the police car, and the cake robbery. When they'd finished, Bert and Nan seemed a little disappointed.

"Nothing else happened?" asked Nan.

"No," said Casey. "We told you everything."

Suddenly the back door swung open. Everyone was startled, until they realized it was one of the workers.

"That's Larry," Casey explained. "He makes deliveries for us."

"Sorry I scared everybody," said the young man. "It's really starting to pour outside, and I didn't want to drip through the front area."

With that, he took off his coat and returned to cleaning up the kitchen.

"Wait a minute!" Flossie said. "The back door was open yesterday morning."

"That's right," said Casey with excitement.

"Maybe the wind blew it open," said Freddie.

"No way," Flossie replied. "I remember there were wet footprints on the floor. Somebody came in through this door."

"Now we're getting somewhere," said Bert. "What happened next?"

Casey thought for a moment. Then she said, "My mom started to pour the cake batter into the pans. And she said that one of the mixers had been turned off."

Flossie ran over to the first mixer. "This is the one," she said.

"What kind of cake was in it?" asked Nan.

"Chocolate," Casey said. "We always use that one for chocolate."

"That's it!" shouted Bert and Nan. They took turns rapidly explaining their deduction.

"Somebody sneaked in here—"

"Probably to hide from the police—"

"Fingers Cranowsky!" said Nan.

"He ran over here—"

"Dropped the key into the batter—"

"Accidentally or on purpose—" Bert added.

"Then ran back out into the alley."

Freddie, Flossie, and Casey stood there in amazement. They kept looking back and forth from Nan, to Bert, then to the mixer.

"But why did he run into this neighborhood?" asked Freddie. "We're nowhere near the places he's been robbing."

"I think I know why," said Nan. "He hid his loot in this area—and I bet it's still here!"

"Where is it?" Freddie asked. He was very excited.

Nan pulled the funny-shaped key from her coat pocket. "The bus station across the street," she said. "That's where we'll find the lock to fit this key!"

"All right," said Bert, snapping his fingers. "Casey, tell your parents what we've discovered. Tell them to call Lieutenant Pike and get him here fast. The rest of us are going over to the bus station."

"Why?" asked Casey.

"Because the Cakenapper hasn't been able to get the key back," Nan explained quickly. "He might be trying to break the lock and run away with the loot. Let's go before we're too late!"

Without another word, the Bobbseys dashed through the bakery and out the front door.

The twins waited for the traffic light to change. Then they raced across the street as fast as they could and burst into the bus station.

"This way," shouted Nan. She led the others to the right and down a long, narrow hallway.

"Where are we going?" Freddie asked.

"To the baggage lockers," Nan answered breathlessly. "I'll bet the number on this key will match a number on one of the lockers!"

The Bobbseys reached the locker area. It took up three walls of a small room. The room was deserted except for the Bobbseys.

Nan read off the number on the key, then they split up and started checking the metal plates on the lockers.

Minutes ticked by. It seemed as if they'd never find the right locker—until Flossie called out, "Quick! It's over here on this wall!"

Nan ran over and inserted the key. Instantly the locker door sprang open. As Freddie and Bert joined them, Flossie pulled out a long canvas bag.

They all held their breath as Freddie unzipped the bag. He reached in and pulled out four smaller bags. When the Bobbseys each opened one, they cheered with joy.

"Money!"

"Jewelry!"

"Real silverware!"

"It's all here," said Flossie.

"Yes, it is," said a deep, scary voice.

The Bobbseys looked up. A short man stood in front of them—blocking the only way out. He wasn't wearing a hood, but the twins knew immediately who he was. The Cakenapper—the North Side burglar—Fingers Cranowsky.

He began moving toward them slowly. "Yes, it's all there. And now nothing stands between me and what's mine. Not even you kids. Especially not you."

10

Just Desserts

Fingers Cranowsky had bushy eyebrows, beady eyes, and a nasty smile. And the Bobbseys were facing him alone. They had no idea when Lieutenant Pike would arrive. Or even if he was coming at all.

"I would have been gone by now, if it weren't for you kids." Fingers took another step toward the twins.

Nan and Bert tried to stall for time. Sooner or later they'd have to make a move.

"But you lost your key at Baker's Bakery," said Nan.

"Yeah," Fingers replied with a sneer. "As you can see, I've been stashing my loot here. Yesterday morning I ducked into the bakery to hide from the cops. Like a jerk, I dropped the key accidentally into that chocolate cake batter."

"That's why you stole that first cake," Bert said. "You hoped the key was inside."

"And when it wasn't," Nan added, "you stole the delivery list and went after the other cakes."

Fingers chuckled softly. "You kids are good. Too good. That's why I sent you that little egg warning. But you didn't listen. Well, it's too late now. I'll just take what's mine and—"

Suddenly Freddie jumped up. "It's *not* yours!" he shouted at the crook. "You stole this stuff. That doesn't make it yours."

"That's right," yelled Flossie. "You're a thief! And we're not going to let you take anything!"

"Why, you little—" Fingers' face turned red with anger. He rushed at the twins, determined to grab his loot.

Suddenly Bert shouted, "Split!" The Bobbseys didn't think twice. Each one grabbed a bag and ran in a different direction. Bert ran to Fingers' left, Nan to his right, and Flossie and Freddie dodged under his grasp. All four children ran back down the hallway and out into the main lobby.

When they reached the waiting area, they quickly ducked into a crowd of teenagers. The Bobbseys moved with the group so that Fingers wouldn't see them. A second after they hid, the crook appeared.

He quickly moved out into the lobby, looking in all directions. The expression on his face hadn't changed. Fingers Cranowsky was angry. Very angry.

"Why don't we just ask for help?" asked Flossie.

"Because," said Nan, "without a police officer to arrest Fingers, he'll get away."

"That's right," Bert agreed. "We've got to find an officer—"

"Or keep Fingers looking for us until Lieutenant Pike shows up."

"Then we'd better do something fast," Freddie said. "Because here comes Fingers."

Freddie was right. The desperate criminal had spotted them and was walking quickly in their direction.

Immediately the Bobbseys started to hurry through the crowd.

"Why isn't he running after us?" asked Flossie. She was holding onto Bert's jacket so she wouldn't lose him.

"Because he doesn't want to attract attention," said Bert. "Come on. Let's duck through these people. Then we'll hide on the other side of that newsstand."

Once again the twins moved quickly. They

pushed through a crowd of bodies and baggage, and ran to the back of the newsstand.

"We can't keep this up forever," said Nan.

"I've got a plan," Bert declared. "Freddie, you—" Bert froze in midsentence. He looked around. "Where's Freddie?"

"He was right behind me when we hid in that last group of people." Flossie's voice was filled with worry.

Bert, Flossie, and Nan peeked out from behind the newsstand. At first they didn't see their brother or Cranowsky. But then—

"There he is!" Nan shouted.

Bert and Flossie looked at where Nan was pointing. Immediately they saw Freddie streak past them, running as fast as he could. Fingers Cranowsky was only a few feet behind him.

Bert took off. "Come on!"

Freddie ran around and through groups of people. He leaped over luggage and slipped under guard rails and signs. But he was barely staying ahead of the thief. Fingers was right behind him and getting closer every second.

And coming up fast behind the crook were the other Bobbseys.

"We have to draw attention to him," Nan said desperately.

"You're right," Bert said between breaths.

The three Bobbseys began shouting:

"Stop, thief!"

"Police!"

"Grab that man, he's a crook!"

People stared in surprise and confusion. They knew something was going on, but they couldn't tell what it was.

Bert, Nan, and Flossie could see Fingers closing in on Freddie. But they weren't close enough to help.

Just as the thief was about to grab Freddie's collar, the young Bobbsey ducked and ran into a coffee shop.

Once inside, Freddie dropped to the floor and began crawling under the tables.

"Hey! What's going on?" yelled a customer.

"Come out of there, young man," called another.

Fingers grabbed for Freddie. But he couldn't reach far enough under the tables.

Clumsily, he began crawling over chairs and customers, trying to catch Freddie.

Then Nan, Bert, and Flossie charged into the coffee shop.

Nan called out, "That man's the North Side burglar!"

"Yeah, stop him! Hold him for the police!" Bert yelled.

"He's trying to get my brother!" Flossie shouted. "Stop him!"

"They're lying!" Fingers yelled back. "I'm their uncle, and they're just misbehaving."

The customers and the owner were very confused. They didn't know who was telling the truth. Then Nan got an idea.

"Look," she shouted. "If he's not a thief, how did we get these?"

Suddenly Nan turned the bag she was carrying upside down. Out spilled diamond rings, gold necklaces, and pearl and emerald earrings.

Bert and Flossie emptied their bags, too, and tossed money and silverware on the tables.

"See?" said Bert. "This is the stuff he stole!"

The people in the restaurant stared at the stolen goods, then at Fingers Cranowsky. Now they believed the Bobbseys, and they moved to make a circle around the thief.

Fingers tried to run. But as he turned toward the door, something hit him square in the face. It was a wedge of blueberry pie.

"Take that!" cried Freddie Bobbsey. "That's for the chocolate cake you threw at me."

Fingers bolted for the exit. For a moment it looked as if he might escape, but he had to stop when he reached the doorway. There stood Lieutenant Pike and Sergeant Franklin. Sergeant Franklin was holding a pair of handcuffs.

"Hope you enjoyed the meal," said Lieutenant Pike.

"Because now it's time to pay the bill," Sergeant Franklin concluded. She slipped the handcuffs on Fingers without any trouble. The thief was too worn out to resist.

A little while later, in Baker's Bakery, the Bobbseys enjoyed a special celebration. The Bakers were throwing a cake-and-cookie party to honor the Bobbsey twins.

The twins and their mother were sitting with Mr. and Mrs. Baker, Casey, and Sergeant Franklin.

"And that's the whole story, Sergeant Franklin," Nan was saying between bites of fresh apple pie. "If Fingers hadn't dropped that key—"

"And if Danny hadn't bitten down on it," said Freddie with a chocolaty grin.

"And if Flossie hadn't come to see the bakery in the first place," Casey added cheerfully.

"We never could have solved this case." Flossie took the last bite of her Double-Double Chocolate Chunky cookie.

"Well," said the policewoman, "you did a good job of tracking him down. But I also have to remind you to—"

"Leave police work to the police," chorused all the twins. "We know."

Mrs. Bobbsey smiled. "Wait till your father

comes home from his trip. He'll be so proud of you all," she said.

"By the way, Bert," said Mr. Baker. "I got a phone call from Lew Sugarman this evening. He apologized for his bad temper—and he asked for his job back."

"Oh?" said Bert. He looked at Mr. Baker with a curious expression.

"Yes," said Mr. Baker. "We're going to give him another chance. He said he had you to thank for it."

Bert was embarrassed, but he tried not to let it show. "It's, uh . . . all in a day's work, sir."

"Well," said Freddie, "everything worked out. We found all the stolen stuff, and we caught the crook."

"And," said Mrs. Bobbsey, "the Bakers were nice enough to give you all these wonderful treats."

"Actually, we had to do it," Mrs. Baker said. Her eyes twinkled behind her gold-rimmed glasses.

"Oh?" said Mrs. Bobbsey.

"Certainly," said Mr. Baker. "We had to make sure that Fingers Cranowsky wasn't the only one who got what he deserved. You know what I mean—his *just desserts.*"